The Big Book of
Berenstain Bears®
Stories

The Big Book of Berenstain Bears® Stories

Stan & Jan Berenstain

Random House
New York

Compilation copyright © 2016 by Berenstain Enterprises, Inc.

All rights reserved. Published in the United States by Random House Children's Books, a division of Penguin Random House LLC, New York.

Random House and the colophon and Bright & Early Books and the colophon are registered trademarks of Penguin Random House LLC.

The stories in this collection were originally published separately in the United States by Random House Children's Books as the following:

Inside, Outside, Upside Down copyright © 1968 by Stanley and Janice Berenstain, renewed 1996

Bears on Wheels copyright © 1969 by Stanley and Janice Berenstain, renewed 1997

He Bear, She Bear copyright © 1974 by Stanley and Janice Berenstain

The Berenstain Bears on the Moon copyright © 1985 by Stanley and Janice Berenstain, renewed 1997

Old Hat, New Hat copyright © 1970 by Stanley and Janice Berenstain

The Bear Detectives copyright © 1975 by Stanley and Janice Berenstain

The Bear Scouts copyright © 1967 by Stanley and Janice Berenstain

Visit us on the Web!
randomhousekids.com
BerenstainBears.com

Educators and librarians, for a variety of teaching tools, visit us at
RHTeachersLibrarians.com

ISBN 978-0-399-55597-8

Library of Congress Control Number: 2015955272

Printed in the United States of America
10 9 8 7 6 5 4 3 2 1

Contents

Inside, Outside, Upside Down   9

Bears on Wheels   39

He Bear, She Bear   73

On the Moon   113

Old Hat, New Hat   155

The Bear Detectives   184

The Bear Scouts   227

The Big Book of
Berenstain Bears® Stories

INSIDE
OUTSIDE
UPSIDE DOWN

Going in

Inside

Inside a box

Upside down

Inside a box
Upside down

Going out

Outside

Outside
Inside a box
Upside down

Going on

On a truck
Outside
Inside a box
Upside down

Going

Going to town
On a truck
Outside
Inside a box
Upside down

Falling off

Off the truck

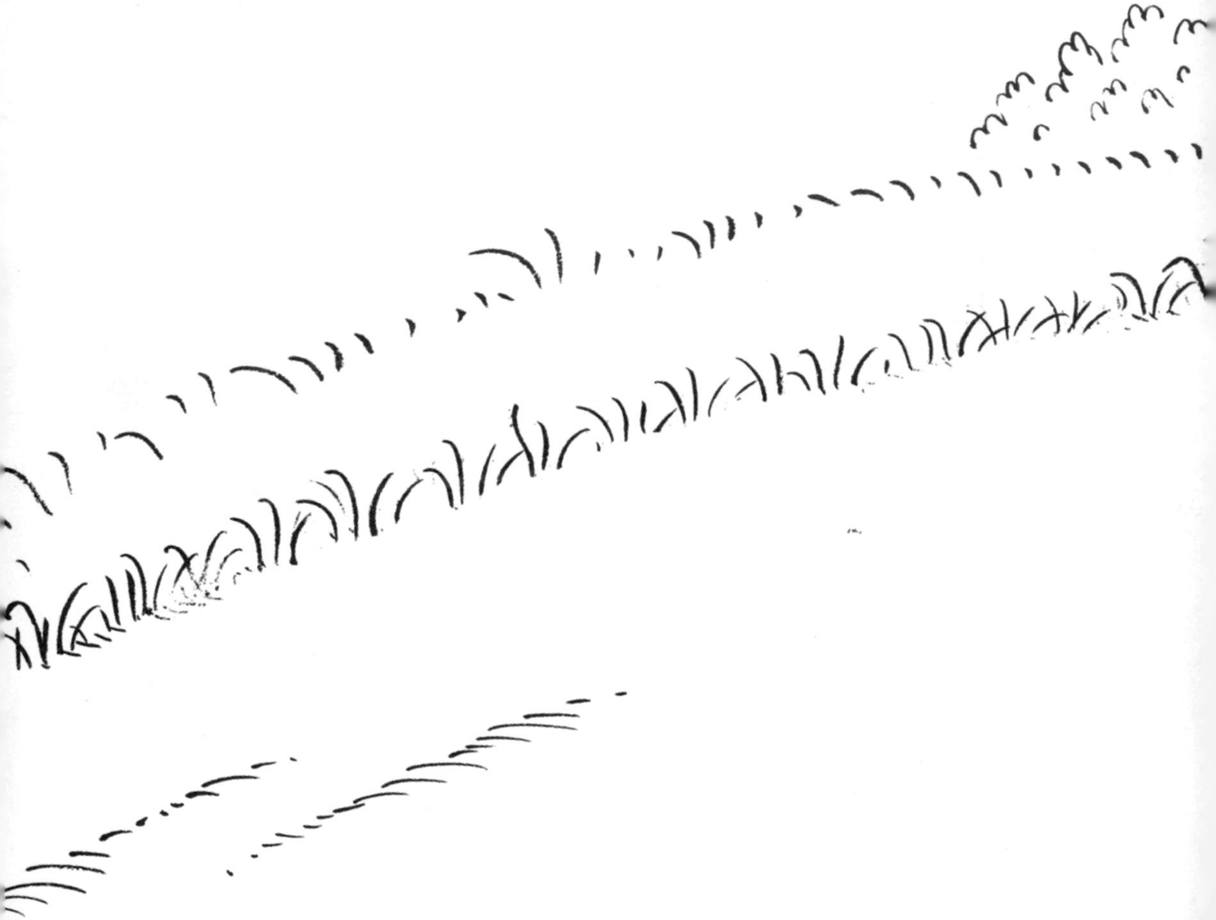

Coming out

Right side up!

Mama! Mama!
I went to town.
Inside,
Outside,
Upside down!

BEARS ON WHEELS

One bear.

One wheel.

One bear on one wheel.

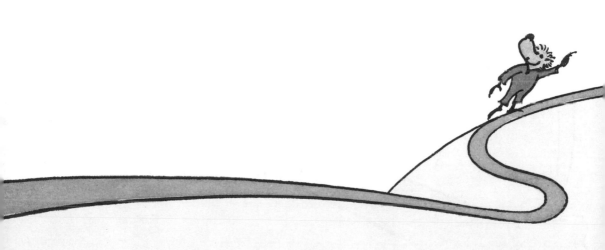

Two bears on one wheel.

Three on one.

Four on one.

Four bears on one wheel.

One bear on two wheels.

Four on two.

One on one again.

One on one.

Three on three.

None on four.

Four on none.

One on one again.

Five on one.

Five bears on one.

Five bears on none.

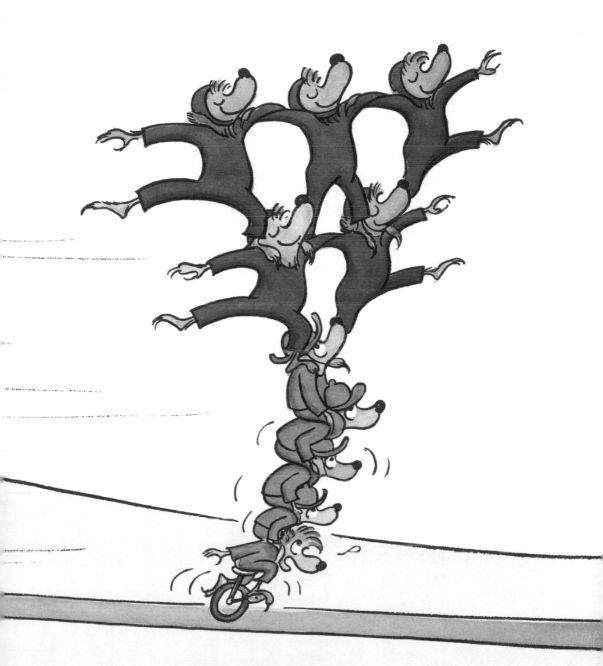

Ten on one.

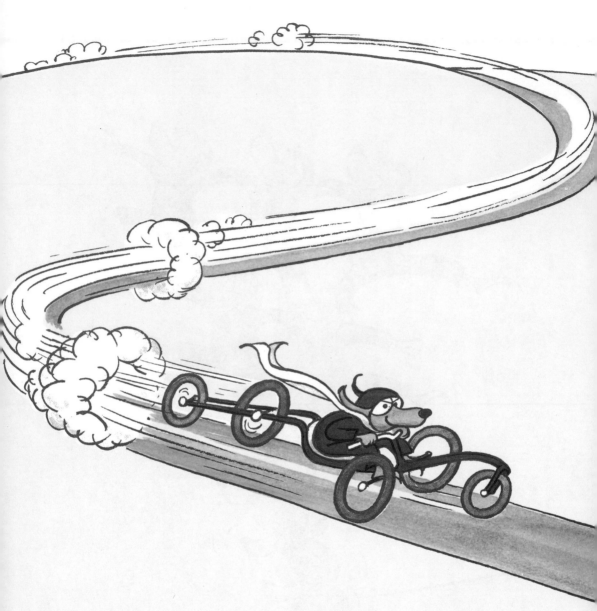

One bear on five wheels.

One on five.

Ten on one.

Ten on ten.

Twenty-one on none.

One on one again.

HE BEAR

SHE BEAR

I see her.
She sees me.

We see that we
are he and she.

Every single
bear we see
is a he bear
or a she.

Every single
bear we see
has lots of things
to do and be.

I'm a father.
I'm a he.
A father's something
you could be.

I'm a mother.
I'm a she.
A mother's something
you could be.

Dad's a he.
Mom's a she.

Those are things
that we could be
just because
we're he and she.

But there are
other things to be.
Come on, He Bear,
follow me!

We could . . .

fix a clock,

paint a door,

BEARTOWN

build a house,

have a store.

bulldoze roads,

drive a train.

We fix clocks,
we paint doors,
we build houses,
we have stores.

We bulldoze roads,
we drive cranes,
we drive trucks,
we drive trains.

We can do all these things,
you see,
whether we are he or she.

87

We climb ladders
to fix the wires.

We climb ladders
to put out fires.

That's Officer Marguerite.
She tells us when
to cross the street.

89

You could . . .
  Be a doctor—
  make folks well.

Teach kids how
to add and spell.

90

Knit a sock,

sew a dress,

paint a picture—

what a mess!

You could . . .

Lead a band,
play a song,
play a tuba,
beat a gong.

Play a banjo—
plink-a-plink.
You could even play
on a kitchen sink.

We have stores,
we fix clocks,
we are officers,
we knit socks.

We teach kids how
to add and spell,
we drive, we build,
we make folks well.

We climb ladders,
we sew dresses,
we make music,
we make messes.

We can do all these things,
you see,
whether we are he or she.

What will we do,
you and I?

I'll tell you what
I'm going to try . . .

I may build bridges,

I may climb poles,

I may race cars,

I may dig holes.

I could be a magician,

I could go on TV,

I could study the fish
who live in the sea.

I'll be a cowboy,

I'll go to the moon,

I'll feed a whale,

I'll train a baboon.

We'll fly a giant
jumbo jet.

We'll build the tallest building yet.

We will jump
on a trampoline.

We'll do tricks
that have never
been seen.

We'll tame
twelve tigers . . .

and twenty-six fleas.

We'll do a dance
on a flying trapeze.

We'll jump and dig
and build and fly. . . .
There's nothing that
we cannot try.

We can do all these things,
you see,
whether we are he OR she.

So many things
to be and do,
He Bear, She Bear,
me . . . and you.

ON THE MOON

On the night before
the Bears' big day,
they look at the moon,
far, far away.

Then morning comes.
Today is the day
they will go to the moon,
far, far away.

10-9-8-7-6-5-4-3-2-1!

The crowd counts down.
The rockets blast.
They wave good-bye.
They are off at last!

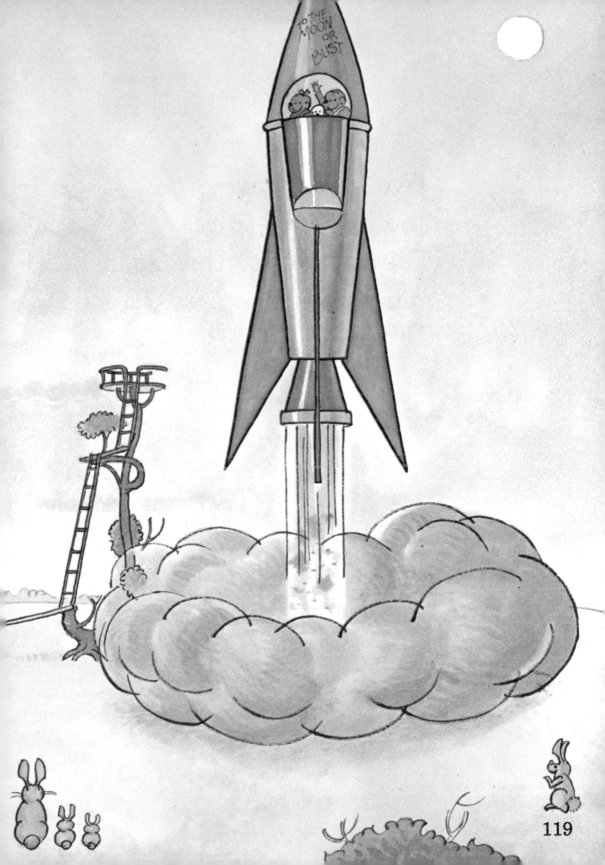

119

Two little bears
and one little pup.
They are off to the moon,
going up, up, up!

They look back down.
But they can't find
their treehouse home.
They have left it far behind.

Where is their town?
It is hard to say.
Their town is now
far, far away.

Now their feet
no longer touch the ground!
They are out in space.
They float around.

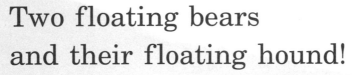

Two floating bears
and their floating hound!

Up ahead!
It's a shower!
It's a meteor shower!
They will have to go through!
Turn on more power!

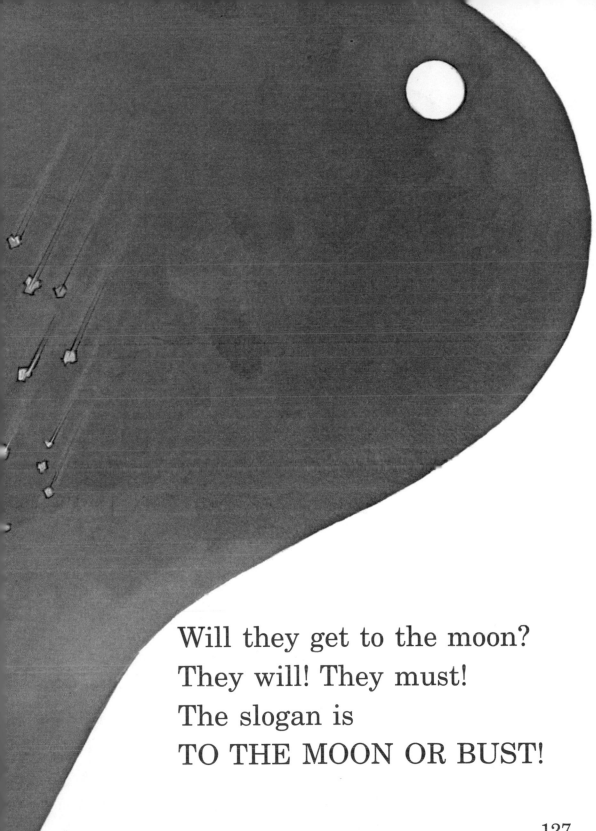

Will they get to the moon?
They will! They must!
The slogan is
TO THE MOON OR BUST!

Behind them, the earth
is now so small
it is nothing more
than a small blue ball.
The pup begins
to wonder when
his paws will touch
the earth again.

Then up ahead,
it's there! The moon!
Buckle up tight!
We are landing soon!

Landing!
They are landing
in a cloud of dust.
They said they would.
And they said they must.
They made it to the moon.
And they didn't bust.

Down onto the old moon
they step with pride.
Two bears
and a pup
along for the ride.

Now the bears
have many things to do.
But first they look around.
They enjoy the view.

137

Then they fly their flag.
They take moon notes.

They collect moon rocks
in their moon rock totes.

Then they try some jumps.
High in the sky.
Moon jumps
almost make you fly!

Now it's time to get
behind the wheel
and explore the moon
in their moonmobile.

Two bears on the moon.
They are all packed up,
ready to go home now.
So is their pup.

Will their ship lift off?
Will the rockets burn?
Will the two little bears
and their pup return?

If the two little bears
use all their skill,
they will return.
They will! They will!

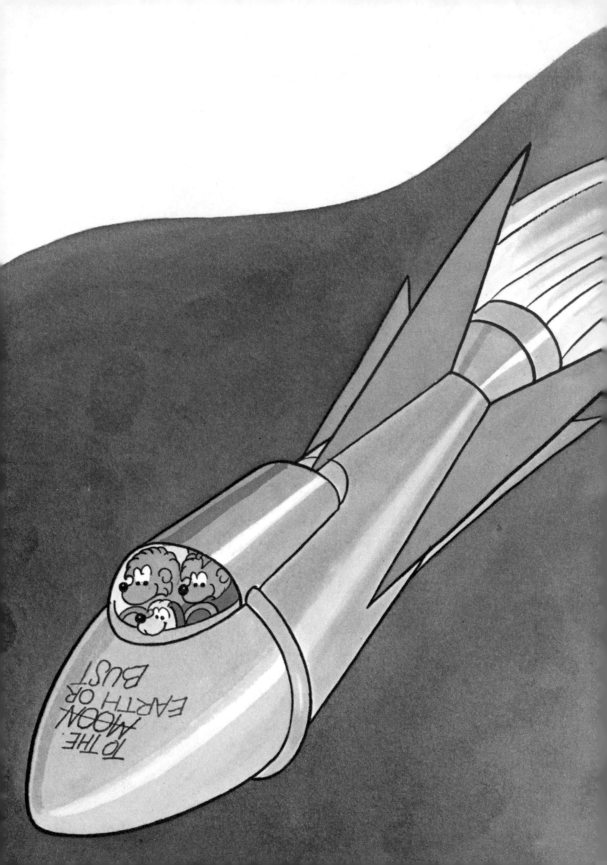

Two bears and their pup
in their rocket ship,
on their way back home
on their back-to-earth trip.

To their friends on the ground!
To their house!
Safe and sound!

Safe back on the earth.
They step out of their ship.
"Wow!" say the bears.
"That was quite a trip!"

Now they look up at the stars,
very, very far away.
Will they go up to a star . . . ?
Well, they may . . . someday.

152

OLD HAT

NEW HAT

Old hat.

Old hat.

New hat.

160

New hat

New hat

New hat

New hat

Too big.

Too small.

Too flat.

Too tall.

Too loose.

Too tight.

Too heavy.

Too light.

Too red.   Too dotty.

Too blue. Too spotty.

Too fancy.

Too frilly.

Too shiny.

Too silly.

Too
beady.

Too
bumpy.

Too
leafy.

Too
lumpy.

Too
holey.

Too
patchy.

Too
feathery.

Too
scratchy.

Too
crooked.

Too
straight.

Too
pointed . . .

WAIT!

Just right!

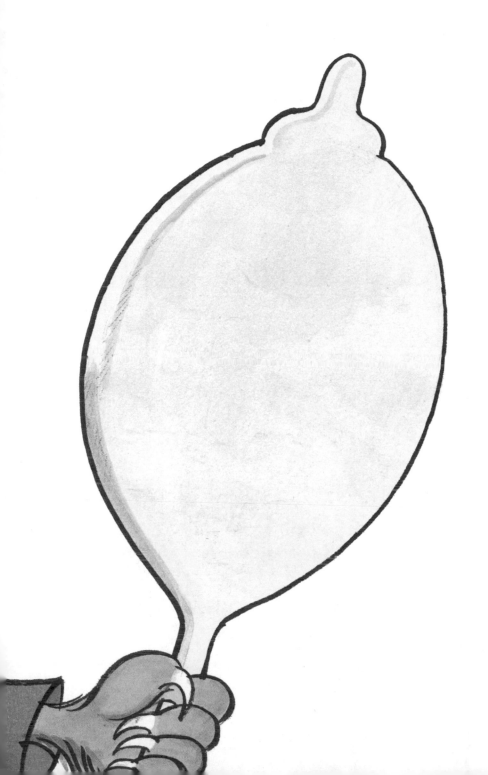

New hat.

Old hat.

THE BEAR

FAIR

DETECTIVES

THE CASE OF THE MISSING PUMPKIN

THE BEAR DETECTIVES

Will they solve the case?

Farmer Ben

Will he get his pumpkin back?

The Missing Pumpkin

Where can it be?

The Spooky Stranger

Who can it be?

Papa Bear
and Snuff

Will they
be much help?

Will the Bear Detectives get their bear?

Help!
My pumpkin won
first prize at the fair.
Now I can't find it
anywhere!

Do not worry,
Farmer Ben.
The BEAR DETECTIVES
will find it again!

Your prize pumpkin stolen?
Never fear.
Great Bear Detective Pop is here!
I will find it.
You will see.

Just watch
my old dog Snuff and me.

But, Papa,
our Bear Detective Book
will tell us how
to catch the crook.

"Lesson One.
First look around
for any TRACKS
that are on the ground."

Don't waste your time
with books and stuff!
We're on the trail!
Just follow Snuff!

We'll catch that crook.
We'll show you how.
Snuff and I
will catch the . . .

. . . cow?

Say! Look down there!
Do you see what I see?

There's a
WHEELBARROW TRACK
going by this tree!

A good detective
writes things down:

"Checked out a cow,
white and brown."

The track ends here.
What shall we do?

We'll look in the book.

It says,
"Lesson Two.
Look all around
for another clue."

Humf! You can look around
as much as you please.
I'm going to follow
these carrots and peas . . .

. . . and eggshells
and corncobs
and other stuff.

This must be the way!
Let's go, Snuff!

MUNCH MUNCH CRUNCH GOBBLE

Listen, Snuff!
Hear that munching?
That pumpkin thief is
pumpkin lunching!

O.K., thief!
You've munched your last.
Your pumpkin-stealing
days are past.

Look here! Look here,
Papa Bear.
We found a new clue
over there.

You see
we found
a PUMPKIN LEAF . . .

Aha!
You've found a pumpkin leaf.
Just show me where
you found this leaf.
Then I will find that
pumpkin thief.

The pumpkin thief!
I've found him, Snuff!
Let's grab him quick.
He sure looks tough.

Be careful, Pop.
Lesson Three in the book
says, "Before you leap,
be sure to look."

Hang on, Snuff!
Hold him tight!
This pumpkin thief
can really fight.

Did you find any clues
in that scarecrow, Pop?
Shall we keep on looking,
or shall we stop?

Hmmmmmmmmmm . . .
Checked out a cow,
three pigs in a pen,
and a scarecrow owned
by Farmer Ben.

Found some tracks
and a pumpkin leaf.
Still haven't found
that pumpkin thief.

Look! By that haystack!
I see something blue!
It's the first-prize ribbon.
That's a very good clue!

A haystack!
The perfect place
to hide.

I'll bet the thief
is right inside.

Pumpkin thief,
don't try to run.
Your pumpkin-stealing
days are done!

But, Papa . . .

I was trying to say,
I don't think the thief
is in THAT hay.

Hmmmmmm . . .
Ben's haystack
is another spot
where the pumpkin thief
is not.

Say! Look over there!
Look in that door!
PUMPKIN SEEDS
all over the floor!

He's in the barn! This is it!
Hand me that detective kit.

I'll snap on these handcuffs.
I'll take him to jail.
Pumpkin thief,
it's the end of the trail.

Old Snuff,
this may be tough.

It looks
like we've caught
a whole GANG
of crooks.

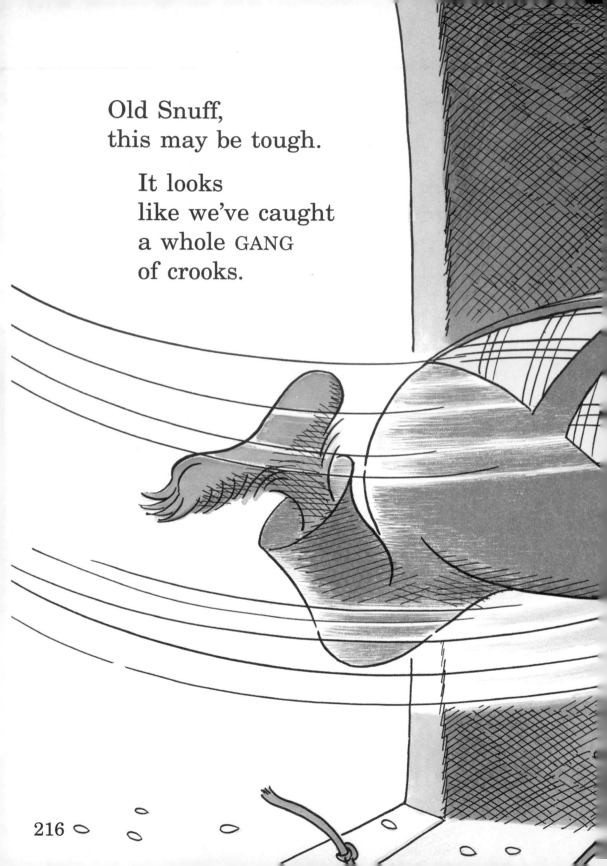

Hmmmmm . . .
Checked out a cow,
brown and white.
Checked out a scarecrow
after a fight.

Checked out a haystack.
Three pigs in a pen . . .
Put the cuffs on
Farmer Ben's hen.

Found some tracks,
a ribbon, a leaf . . .
some pumpkin seeds,

BUT STILL
NO THIEF!

Small Bear, I guess you better look
at what it says there in your book.

Lesson Four—
here's how it goes—
"A good detective
will USE HIS NOSE!"

Hmmmmmmm . . .
Pumpkin seeds,
pumpkin shell—
and . . .
aha!
I smell a
PUMPKIN SMELL!

The pumpkin was pied
by Mrs. Ben.

The case is solved.
Good work, men!
The BEAR DETECTIVES
have done it again!

MMMMMMM!
My dear, you and I
will SHARE first prize,
ME for the pumpkin,
YOU for the pies!

The Bear Scouts

Good-bye, Bear Scouts!
Good luck! Have fun!
Isn't Dad going camping
with you, Son?

Not this time.
We don't need Pa.
We've got the Bear Scout
Guidebook, Ma.
It tells us all
we need to know
about camping out
and whcre to go.

A guidebook, Son?
Now, wait a minute!
I know more
than the book has in it.

A smart bear opens
his eyes wide
and never needs
a Bear Scout Guide.

Now, Son, stop.
Right here you'll see
just why you need
a guide like me!

What would you do,
my fine young scout,
to get across
when a bridge is out?

The book says first,
"In such a spot . . .

tie your rope
with a Bear Scout knot."

Scout knot—bah!
A smart bear knows
he has no need
for one of those.
He ties his own knot
to the tree
and safely crosses.
Now watch me.

We're here, Scouts.
But Dad is not!
What has happened
to his knot?

On second thought—
I'll stay with you.
So I can show you
what to do.
That camp ground is so far,
you see,
you really need
a guide like me.

Look here, Bear Scouts.
Your book can't show
which way is
the way to go.
But a bear like me,
a bear who's clever,
takes the short way.
The long way? Never!

But, Papa, wait!

Here's a map in the book.

It says to go

the long way. Look!

Well, you'll find me
at the other end.
A smart bear takes
the short way, friend.

On second thought,
I'll come along.
Just in case
something goes wrong.

Now that I've brought you
safely here,
we'll get down this river.
Never fear.

Yes, Papa. Look.

Here's a plan in the book.

It shows us all

we need to do . . .

To build a fine
Bear Scout canoe.

Build a canoe?

That takes too long!

A bear who's smart

will know that's wrong.

It's easy to see

that's much too slow.

I know a faster

way to go.

So long, Bear Scouts!
Toodle-oo!
You can have
your slow canoe.

I never like
to wait around.
I'll meet you
at the camping ground.

We're coming, Dad!
Just grab the rope.
The Guidebook says
there's always hope.

On second thought—
I'll go with you.
Then I can show you
what to do.
If you go on
and I do not,
you'll never find
your camping spot.

You won't need
the Guidebook now.
Here's where I really
show you how.
For this is where
we set up camp,
and I'm the world's
camp set-up champ!

BEAR SCOUT
CAMPING
GROUND

Now watch this.
I'm really good
at starting a fire
by rubbing wood.

263

Excuse me, Dad.

That way's not right.

The book says

that will take all night.

We'll try this way.
It ought to light.
Look! Now our fire
is burning bright.

Bear Scouts, you're
going to have a treat.
I'll cook you something
good to eat.

A wise bear knows
there's a meal to be found
wherever he is,
if he just looks around.

I'll put in some eggs
and fresh green weeds.
Some toadstools. Then
some roots and leaves.
And presto, chango,
ala kazoo . . .
That's how I make
my favorite stew.

Dad, your stew
is stewing well.
But doesn't it have
a funny smell?

Besides, the book says,
"For the best camp dish,
take your rods
and catch some fish."

On second thought—
I'll share your meal.
My stew's a bit
too rich, I feel.

Now, Scouts, you'll find
a bear who's bright
will make his bed
while it's still light.

276

The Guidebook says—
page eighty-eight—
"Put up your tents
before it's late."

Tents are for sissies!
Be smart, be brave!
You haven't camped out
till you've slept
in a cave.

Ow! That was quite
a fall I took.
You'd better come
and
BRING
THAT
BOOK!

We're coming, Dad.
No need to worry.
We'll have you mended
in a hurry.

First, bandage nose,
then thumb, then head.
Then put me
on a rescue sled.

Well done, Bear Scouts!
We're nearly there,
thanks to your
smart old Papa Bear.
As I have told you
all along,
with a guide like me,
you can't go wrong.

Dad has shown us
quite a lot
about what's smart
and what is not.

Stan & Jan Berenstain

were successful cartoonists for magazines and humor books when they began writing for children. Their first story starring the bear family, *The Big Honey Hunt,* appeared in 1962. Since then, more than 360 Berenstain Bears books have been published, and more than 300 million copies have been sold. What began as an idea sparked by their young sons' love of reading has become one of the best-loved—and bestselling—children's book series of all time.

BEGINNER BOOKS
by the Berenstains

The Bear Detectives

The Bears' Picnic

The Bears' Vacation

The Berenstain Bears and
the Missing Dinosaur Bone

The Big Honey Hunt

BRIGHT & EARLY BOOKS
by the Berenstains

Bears in the Night

The Berenstain Bears and
the Spooky Old Tree

The Bike Lesson

He Bear, She Bear

Inside, Outside, Upside Down

Old Hat, New Hat

Now that you've finished this book, be sure to read . . .

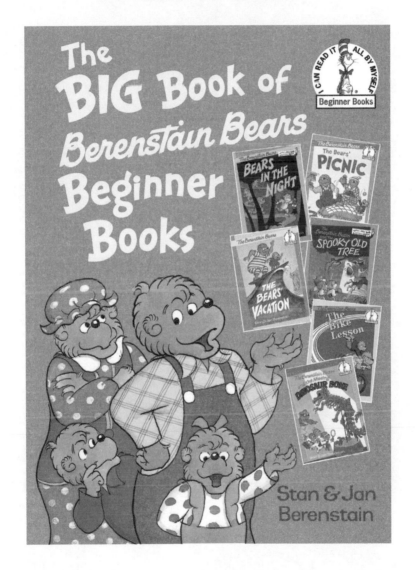